The Moon Was the Best

Donald McKay School

The Moon Was the Best

By Charlotte Zolotow

Photographs by Tana Hoban

Greenwillow Books, New York

The full-color photographs were reproduced from 35-mm slides.
The text type is Berkeley Old Style Medium.

Printed in Singapore by Tien Wah Press
First Edition   10 9 8 7 6 5 4 3

Library of Congress Cataloging-in-Publication Data

Zolotow, Charlotte (date)
The moon was the best / by Charlotte Zolotow ;
photographs by Tana Hoban.
p.   cm.
Summary: A mother visiting Paris brings back to her
daughter all her best memories, of the beautiful
fountains, the sparkling Seine, parks like paintings,
and paintings like parks.
ISBN 0-688-09940-8 (trade). ISBN 0-688-09941-6 (lib.)
[1. Paris (France)—Fiction.
2. Mothers and daughters—Fiction.]
I. Hoban, Tana, ill.   II. Title.
PZ7.Z77Mo   1993
[E]—dc20
91-47748   CIP   AC

WHERE THE PHOTOGRAPHS WERE TAKEN

Girl with balloons (on jacket and cover): Place des Vosges   □   Girl with hoop; man feeding pigeons; painter; carousel: Jardin du Luxembourg   □   Rainbow: buildings on Right Bank of Seine, from Quai de Bourbon   □   Man walking; bookstalls: Left Bank of Seine   □   Woman with bread: Marais district   □   Horse fountain: Fontaine de l'Observatoire in Jardin de l'Observatoire   □   Bridge at night: Pont de la Tournelle

For Robert Warren, with love

— C H A R L O T T E   Z O L O T O W

With love to John, who gave me Paris

— T A N A   H O B A N

Once a mother and father were going to Paris.
"Remember the special things to tell me," said
the little girl, "the things I'd like if I were there."
So the mother remembered.

She remembered the flowering chestnut trees
along the streets and how strange it was to be
wakened by birds in the middle of a city.

She remembered how the sky
showed everywhere because
the buildings were low.

She remembered the river Seine
and how, going from one side of Paris
to the other, you could always
see it sparkling in the sun.

She remembered the man feeding

a cluster of silvery pigeons

every morning when she passed.

She remembered the bookstalls
lined against the old stone wall
above the banks of the river.

She remembered how the people carried
long loaves of unwrapped bread,
like sticks under their arms.

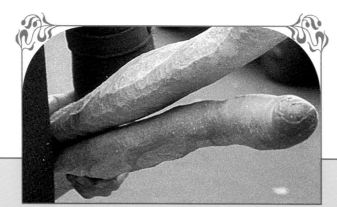

She remembered parks like paintings

and paintings like parks.

She remembered how people sat at outdoor cafes

while underneath the tables

the dogs watched everyone go by.

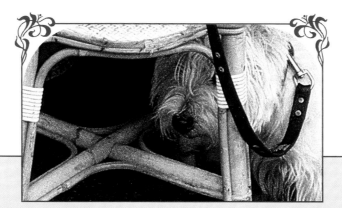

She remembered a tiny carousel,

like a birthday cake, with

white animals waiting for the music to start.

She remembered how there were flowers everywhere,

in all the stores, in every house, even

in the window of the corner butcher shop.

She remembered how the fountains
sprayed water in a curving white mist
over prancing horses and glistening gods.

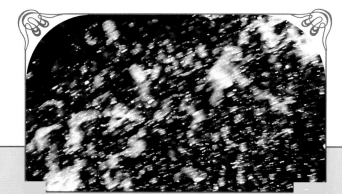

She remembered how the city at night
was like magic with the trees whispering
and the river reflecting the lights
and the moon in the sky.

"What was the best?" the little girl asked.

"Oh," said her mother, "the moon was the best

because it was the same moon shining on you,

so I knew we weren't far apart at all."